Itty ♥ Bitty PRINCESS Kitty

3

The Puppy Prince

by Melody Mews ★ illustrated by Ellen Stubbings

LITTLE SIMON

New York London Toronto Sydney New Delhi

LITTLE SIMON

An imprint of Simon & Schuster Children's Publishing Division
1230 Avenue of the Americas, New York, New York 10020
First Little Simon paperback edition May 2020. Copyright © 2020 by Simon & Schuster, Inc.
All rights reserved, including the right of reproduction in whole or in part in any form.
LITTLE SIMON is a registered trademark of Simon & Schuster, Inc., and associated colophon is a trademark of Simon & Schuster, Inc. For information about special discounts for bulk purchases, please contact Simon & Schuster Special Sales at 1-866-506-1949 or business@simonandschuster.com.
The Simon & Schuster Speakers Bureau can bring authors to your live event.
For more information or to book an event contact the Simon & Schuster Speakers Bureau at 1-866-248-3049 or visit our website at www.simonspeakers.com.
Designed by Laura Roode. The text of this book was set in Banda.
Manufactured in the United States of America 0421 MTN 10 9 8 7 6 5 4 3
Cataloging-in-Publication Data is available for this title from the Library of Congress.
ISBN 978-1-5344-6358-5 (hc)
ISBN 978-1-5344-6357-8 (pbk)
ISBN 978-1-5344-6359-2 (eBook)

Contents

The Announcement Dragon

Itty Bitty Princess Kitty was concentrating very hard. Her legs twitched as she focused on the platform across from her. It was so far away! But she'd seen her parents, the Queen and King of Lollyland, make this jump many times.

You can do this, Itty told herself.

Just then, something outside the window caught her eye. She blinked hard.

Was that . . . a *dragon*?

Itty leaped down and raced out of the climbing room. She skidded to a stop in the grand hall, where her parents were standing in front of the palace doors.

"Mom! Dad!" Itty took a deep breath. "There's a DRAGON outside! Run!"

Queen Kitty smiled. "Yes, darling," she purred. "No need to worry—or run. It's an announcement dragon from Wagmire!"

"An announcement dragon?" Itty squeaked. In Lollyland, announcements were made by fairies. Tiny fairies who blew miniature trumpets and did not like to be kept waiting.

The doors opened and a huge dragon entered. He bowed gracefully. And then, to Itty's surprise, the dragon began to sing!

"Greetings from the royal family of Wagmire.
The King, Queen, and Pip are excited to visit Lollyland. . . ."

The dragon paused dramatically. *"They can't wait to see yooooou!"*

With that, the dragon handed the King a scroll, bowed again, and flew away.

"They arrive in two days!" the King boomed after reading the scroll.

"That doesn't give us much time to prepare!" the Queen exclaimed.

"Who is Pip?" Itty asked.

"We must make lists!" the Queen cried.

"Who is Pip?" Itty repeated.

"There's no time for lists!" the King replied.

"WHO IS PIP?" Itty yelled.

That got their attention. Itty knew it wasn't polite to yell, but sometimes a kitty had to be loud to be heard.

"Pip is Prince of Wagmire," her mother explained. "He's your age. I'm sure you will get along marvelously."

A prince was coming to Lollyland? Itty couldn't wait to tell her friends!

Gossip in Goodie Grove

A little while later, the Lollyland mermaids sang three notes, which meant it was almost time for Itty to meet her friends.

Itty raced out the door. Luckily, there was a low-hanging cloud nearby. Itty whistled. As the cloud settled to the ground, she jumped aboard.

"To Goodie Grove!"

Slowly the cloud drifted up and away. Itty loved traveling by cloud. The cloud she was on was very fluffy, so her ride was slow. The gray rain clouds moved superfast—for good reason!—but today was a beautiful sunny day.

Finally the cloud parked at Goodie Grove and Itty climbed out. The air smelled like strawberries, bubble gum, and birthday cake. Goodie Grove was home to the most delicious treats in Lollyland.

Luna Unicorn, Chipper Bunny, and Esme Butterfly were already there, munching on marshmallow sticks.

"Sorry I'm late," Itty said.

"That's okay." Luna handed Itty a marshmallow stick.

Itty grinned. Luna always remembered to get an extra treat for a friend.

"I have exciting news," Itty said between bites of gooey marshmallow. "The royal family of Wagmire is coming to Lollyland! Including a prince named Pip!"

"Best. News. Ever!" Luna squealed. Itty, Chipper, and Esme waited for the spray of glitter that always came from Luna's horn when she was excited.

And waited some more.

"Are you out of glitter?" Chipper asked.

"No, I've been practicing," Luna said. "I can control it if I . . ." Luna giggled and a stream of glitter spurted out. "Oopsie! If I concentrate," she finished.

"Luckily, we love glitter," Itty laughed.

"Tell us about Prince Pip," Luna said a moment later.

"I don't know much about him yet," Itty admitted. "But I want his visit to be perfect."

"We can show him around Lollyland," Esme suggested.

"And bring him to our favorite places," Chipper added.

"Great ideas!" Itty nodded. "I'll share my climbing structure with him and get kitty treats of every flavor."

"What if he's not a cat?" Esme asked.

Itty paused. She hadn't thought of that. "Well, that's okay. Everyone likes kitty treats and climbing, right?"

The Castle Prepares

On the cloud ride home, Itty thought more about the prince's visit. Her friends had reminded her that, actually, *not* everyone loved climbing and kitty treats. Itty needed to find out more about Prince Pip.

Inside the palace, preparations were already underway. The royal decorators, a trio of stylish penguins, were near the royal dining room. Itty headed over to say hello and ask if they had seen her mom.

"Hello, Princess!" exclaimed the head decorator penguin. "The Queen is outside with Mr. Bobtail. They are about to unveil the royal guesthouse."

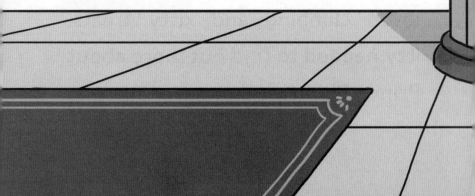

"Thank you!" Itty said with a smile. She didn't want to be late! Mr. Bobtail was the royal architect. With a little help from him, the royal guesthouse could be magically transformed into the

perfect home for its guests. Itty
had seen it turned into a rain forest
tree house for her jaguar cousins
and a sleek, modern cave for a bear
friend of the Queen's. Seeing the
guesthouse transformed should
tell her a lot about the prince!

Itty joined her mom just as the royal architect was having his bird assistants remove the tarp from the guesthouse. Itty held her breath. The guesthouse was revealed and it was . . .

A massive doghouse!

That meant the royal family of Wagmire was a family of dogs. And that the prince was a puppy!

The doghouse was impressive. It was a shimmering gold-plated structure, and the roof sparkled with gemstones shaped like dog bones.

Itty realized her friends were right—this prince probably would not like climbing or eating kitty treats. Itty tried to think of what a puppy might enjoy instead. She knew dogs liked to dig holes and run around. Didn't they like to chase cats? Well, she'd try not to think about that.

Itty was glad she had a couple of days to come up with ideas. She had to make sure the puppy prince had the best time in Lollyland!

The Prince of Wagmire

Itty couldn't believe the day was finally here! The King and Queen had just finished their inspection of the royal guesthouse. The royal family of Wagmire was due to arrive any moment.

"Itty, it was so thoughtful of

you to have a dog bone dispenser placed in the prince's room," the Queen said.

"Well, I love my bedroom treat dispenser, so I thought Pip would like having one too."

That wasn't the only thing Itty had done to make the prince feel comfortable. She'd also stocked his room with every book she could think of that a puppy might enjoy. She hoped Pip liked to read as much as she did.

"I think that's them!" the King cried, pointing to the sky. Itty looked up and saw an enormous spaceship hovering above. As it got closer, Itty realized it wasn't a spaceship at all. It was a giant, flying dog bed!

"That's what I call traveling in style!" Itty exclaimed as the dog bed came to a gentle stop on the palace lawn.

A few moments later, the royal
family of Wagmire emerged. Itty
stood on her tippy-toes, trying to
get a better look at Prince Pip.

"Welcome to Lollyland!" Itty's mom said warmly. "This is King Kitty, and this is our daughter, Itty Bitty Princess Kitty."

Itty smiled and curtsied. "It's nice to meet you," she said. "You can call me Itty. All my friends do."

"Pleasure to meet you, Itty," the King of Wagmire said.

"Please meet our son, Prince Pip of Wagmire," said the Queen of Wagmire. "She can call you Pip, though. Right, honey?"

Pip bowed stiffly. "Nice to meet you, Princess Itty," he said. "I think princes and princesses should always use their royal titles," he added.

"Oh, okay. That's fine. Welcome to Lollyland, Prince Pip," Itty replied. She waited for the prince to say something else, but apparently that was all he had to say.

A Not-So-Perfect Day

As the sun rose the next morning, Itty stretched sleepily. It had taken her a while to fall asleep. She'd been worrying about getting off on the wrong paw with the prince. But today was a new day, and she would fix whatever had happened.

"After breakfast I'll take you on a tour of Lollyland," Itty said to Pip. "And you can meet my friends."

"A day of exploring?" Prince Pip considered it. "I guess that sounds okay."

"You'll love it!" Itty promised.

But later, as Itty and Pip arrived at Starfish Falls, she knew the prince had not loved *anything* so far.

First there had been his reaction to traveling by cloud.

"Is this a royal transportation vehicle?" he'd asked.

"Nope," Itty had replied. "Everyone in Lollyland travels by cloud. I bet it's just like flying on your dog bed!"

"I doubt that," the prince replied. "Our hovercraft has the latest technology. And only the royal family uses it."

Then, when the cloud landed at Goodie Grove, the prince wouldn't get off.

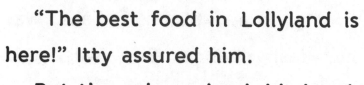

"The best food in Lollyland is here!" Itty assured him.

But the prince shook his head. "I prefer food from the royal kitchen."

Itty knew Starfish Falls was her last chance. She was glad her friends were there. It was impossible not to have fun with Esme, Luna, and Chipper around.

Itty introduced her friends to the prince.

"It's nice to meet you," Luna said in a serious voice.

"Luna, are you okay?" Itty asked.

Luna darted away. Moments later, they heard the "poof" sound of a glitter explosion. "Sorry!" Luna called. "I didn't want to glitter the prince!"

Itty and her friends laughed. Even the prince smiled a little.

"Let's go swimming!" Chipper exclaimed. As her friends raced to the water, Itty turned to Pip. "The water here is always the perfect temperature. And . . ." Itty paused. Now Pip was frowning. "Oh, do you not want to swim?"

Pip shook his head. "A prince must not mess up his fur. Are you sure you want to get *yours* all dirty and wet?"

Itty *was* sure she didn't mind getting her fur wet. But she *wasn't* sure she should leave the prince. Then again, her friends

were having so much fun! She
asked Pip, "Do you mind if I take
a quick dip before we head back?"

The prince shrugged. "I'll wait
here."

It All Makes Sense

After a short swim with her friends, Itty hurried back to Pip, who was just where she had left him. Only now he was reading a book.

"Is that a book from your room?" Itty asked, hoping Pip would say he loved the books she had chosen.

"No. This is the royal rule book. Is it time to go back now?"

"Sure," Itty replied. She waved goodbye to her friends and hailed the nearest cloud.

Itty and Pip rode in silence for a few moments. The prince continued to read while Itty tried to think of something to say.

"When I became princess a few weeks ago, I didn't get a royal rule book. When did you get yours?"

The prince looked up and, for the first time since Itty had met him, he had a huge smile on his face. "You became a princess a few weeks ago? And you didn't get a royal rule book? That explains it!"

"It does?" Itty asked.

"Yes, of course!" Pip nodded excitedly. "Now it all makes sense!"

"It does?" Itty repeated.

Pip's tail wagged. "I've been a prince for a year, so I know all the rules. But if you just became a princess, and didn't receive a royal rule book, then *of course* you wouldn't know how to act like a princess!"

Itty wasn't sure what to say. Did Pip think she didn't know how to act like a princess? She couldn't help but feel upset. But this was the happiest she'd seen Pip, and he was her guest, after all.

"So, um, what do you mean I don't act like a princess?" Itty asked.

"It's all in here," Pip said, handing the book to Itty. "Now that you're a princess, you can't do normal kitty things like ride in clouds and swim at the falls. But don't worry, Princess Itty. My rule book will teach you everything you need to know."

♥ chapter 7 ♥

The Royal Rule Book

That night Itty read Pip's rule book before bed. It wasn't very much fun to read, but Itty had promised Pip. She tossed and turned all night, thinking about the royal rules.

A princess must always wear royal attire.

A princess
must never
mess up
her fur.

A princess
shall not do
chores.

And there were many, many more rules.

When it was time to get ready for school the next morning, instead of choosing one of the simple dresses she usually wore, Itty selected a velvet gown.

"Itty, are you sure you want to
wear that fancy dress to school?"
the Queen asked gently.

Pip, who was seated next to Itty finishing his breakfast, smiled at her. Itty smiled back.

"Mom, a princess must always wear royal attire."

The Queen was about to respond, but just then, the Lollyland mermaids sang eight notes. "Time for school!" the King announced. "Itty, did you make your bed?"

"Um, no," Itty said. "A princess shall not do chores."

The King and Queen both frowned. "Itty, you know you are responsible for making your bed," said the Queen.

Itty didn't know what to say, so she gathered her things and headed for school.

The rest of Itty's day wasn't any easier than breakfast had been. At recess, she realized she couldn't play on the slide or run around. Her gown was way too stiff. Not to mention itchy.

"Itty, why are you dressed like that?" Luna asked.

"It's royal attire," Itty explained.

"Are you going to change for Goodie Grove after school?" Chipper asked.

Itty shook her head. "I can't go to Goodie Grove. It's not a royally approved location."

"But you always hang out with us after school," Esme said, seeming a little sad.

"Itty, what's going on?" Luna asked. "You're not acting like yourself."

As Itty looked at each of her friends, she had to admit . . . she didn't *feel* like herself one bit.

♥ chapter 8 ♥

Itty's Royal Rules

So Itty went to Goodie Grove with her friends. But she only stayed for a bit. She had to get home and do her chores. Plus, she wanted to talk to Pip.

When Pip saw Itty, he noticed her gown was splattered with

maple syrup from her trip to
Goodie Grove.

"Your royal attire!" he cried.

"I have something to show you.
Come with me," Itty said to Pip.

Itty took Pip up to her room. She invited him to sit on her magic beanbag chair.

"This doesn't look like a royal throne," Pip said.

"Just try it!" Itty replied.

The prince looked a little unsure, but he finally sat in the chair.

"Oohh, this is comfy," he said as he sank into the squishy beans. But then he sprang to his feet. "I don't think that's a royal chair. Let me check my book. . . ."

"Pip," Itty said, and when she noticed Pip frowning, she began again. "*Prince* Pip, I tried following all the rules today and it was . . . terrible. How do you ever have any fun?"

"Princes don't get to have fun," Pip replied. "You just don't understand yet. I *used* to have fun, before I became a prince. I had diving contests into Magic Mountain Lake with my friends

and we'd explore secret areas of Wagmire and—" The prince stopped himself. The things he used to do weren't meant for a prince. "Never mind. That was the *old* me. This is the *new* me."

"But that's silly!" Itty exclaimed. "There are no rules that say you can't have fun!"

Pip shrugged.

Itty could tell Pip didn't believe her. She looked around her room and suddenly had an idea.

Itty walked over to the case that held her shooting star. It glowed softly. "This shooting star made me a princess," Itty told Pip. "The day it arrived was the best day of my life."

"It's beautiful," Pip said.

"Thank you," Itty replied. She looked at her star and spoke from her heart. "I love being a princess," she told Pip. "But I'm the kind of princess *I* want to be. One who does regular kitty things, like play with my friends and ride on clouds. And I . . . I don't think that makes me a bad princess."

There, she'd said it.

Pip sank back into the magic beanbag chair. "Wearing royal attire all the time *is* pretty uncomfortable," he admitted. "It's hot."

"And itchy!" Itty added.

Pip laughed.

"Prince Pip," Itty began, "what would happen if you didn't follow *every* rule in your rule book?"

"I have no idea," Pip said with a shrug. Then he smiled. "But I'm willing to find out!"

Do-Over Day

The next day Pip and Itty had a plan. They were going to have a do-over day and Itty would show Pip around Lollyland again.

"Let's catch a cloud!" Pip exclaimed as soon as breakfast was over.

Pip was so excited when they got to Goodie Grove that Itty and her friends could barely keep up with him.

"What do you think of Lollyland syrup?" Esme asked as Pip sampled a third flavor.

"It's delicious!" Pip shouted excitedly. The syrup fairy nodded in approval.

"It's *almost* as delicious as Wagmire syrup," Pip added.

"HRRRMPH! Excuse me?" The syrup fairy threw down her wand and stomped away.

"Oh no!" Pip cried. "Sorry! I meant to say it's *just as* delicious."

"We'd better go before she tells the other fairies." Itty giggled. So they jumped off their candy rocks and hurried away.

"Seems like a good time for a dip at Starfish Falls!" Pip said happily.

Pip loved swimming at Starfish Falls even more than Itty expected. After saying goodbye to Luna, Chipper, and Esme, Itty decided there was time for one more stop on Pip's tour.

"This is downtown Lollyland,"
Itty explained as they hopped off
their cloud. "All the shops, offices,
and restaurants are here. Can you
guess what my favorite shop is?"

Pip looked around the bustling main street. He pointed to Bunny's Best Books.

"Yup! You guessed right!" Itty beamed. "Let's go inside. This is Chipper's family's store!"

Inside the store, Chipper's mom and dad happily greeted Itty.

"This is my friend, Prince Pip," Itty said.

"It's a pleasure to meet you, Prince Pip." Mr. and Mrs. Bunny bowed.

"I love your store!" Pip replied. "And please call me Pip." He exchanged a smile with Itty. "All my friends do."

♥ chapter 10 ♥

Friends
Forever

Later that day Itty and Pip headed
to the royal dining room for the
farewell feast.

"I wish I could have worn
regular clothes," Pip whispered.

"Doesn't a feast require royal
attire?" Itty asked with a laugh.

But Itty and Pip forgot all about their uncomfortable royal clothing when they saw the delicious food on gleaming silver platters. It was truly a feast fit for two kings, two queens, a prince, and a princess.

Just before dessert, Pip's parents raised their bowls of water. "We would like to thank you for this visit," the King said. "You have made us feel so welcome. Please promise to visit us in Wagmire!"

A little while later, Itty and Pip changed into their comfiest clothes before going on one last playdate with Esme, Chipper, and Luna.

Pip told them all about Wagmire.

"I've been meaning to ask you," Itty said. "If there's no cloud travel in Wagmire, how does everyone get around?"

"Submarines," Pip replied.

"*What?*" Itty, Luna, Chipper, and Esme exclaimed at the same time.

Pip laughed. "Wagmire has a lot of water, so submarine travel is the fastest way to get around."

"Now I really want to visit!" Itty said excitedly. "Are there any royal events coming up?"

"Actually . . . there's a royal ball next month," Pip said slowly.

"That's exciting!" Luna cried.

Pip shook his head. "Not really. I don't know how to dance."

"Oh, that's okay," Itty assured him. "I just attended my first royal ball. I had to come up with my own steps to a new dance, and I was so nervous because I didn't want to mess up!"

"What did you do?" Pip asked.

"Well, my friends helped me a lot." Itty grinned at Esme, Chipper, and Luna. "And then when the time came, there was sort of a . . . happy accident," Itty said.

Pip raised his eyebrows.

"I'll explain another time," Itty said with a smile. "But for the rest of the ball, I just did what felt natural on the dance floor. I realized it was easiest to dance whatever way felt right to me."

"Dancing how it feels right to me," Pip repeated. "I think I can do that," he said, and then he shook his tail. Everyone laughed.

Itty was really glad to see that her *new* friend had found his *old* self again.

1.
A prince/princess shall ~~NOT~~ play with their food.

2.
A prince/princess shall ~~NOT~~ tell jokes.

3.
A prince/princess shall ~~NOT~~ get their clothes dirty.

4.

A prince / princess shall ~~NOT~~ go to non-royal locations.

5.

A prince/princess shall ~~NOT~~ play games.

Here's a sneak peek at Itty's next royal adventure!

Knock-knock-knock.

Someone was knocking on Itty's open bedroom door. It was the Queen of Lollyland, also known as Itty's mother.

"I came to remind you to tidy up your closet, but I see you beat me to it!" Queen Kitty said with a smile.

"Almost done!" Itty exclaimed.

"I'll see you soon for breakfast then, darling," the Queen replied.

Even though Itty was the princess of Lollyland, she still had to do chores, like tidying up her closet when it was messy.

Her closet had *definitely* been messy after Itty's friend Luna had left yesterday. The girls had played dress-up, and most of

Itty's clothes had landed on the floor. But now everything was back where it belonged.

Something still isn't right, Itty thought. She looked more closely. Her dresses were on hangers, and her shoes were neatly stacked on the shoe rack.

What can it be? Itty wondered. And then she realized exactly what it was. Her tiara. It was gone!